Leila 🐾 Nugget

MYSTERY

The Case with No Clues

Deserae and Dustin Brady

Illustrations by April Brady

Andrews McMeel
PUBLISHING®

Other Books by Dustin Brady

Escape from a Video Game: The Secret of Phantom Island

Escape from a Video Game: Mystery on the Starship Crusader

Escape from a Video Game: The Endgame

Trapped in a Video Game

Trapped in a Video Game: The Invisible Invasion

Trapped in a Video Game: Robots Revolt

Trapped in a Video Game: Return to Doom Island

Trapped in a Video Game: The Final Boss

Superhero for a Day

Leila and Nugget Mystery: Who Stole Mr. T?

CONTENTS

BURIED TREASURE

"Thanks, Miss Carol!" Leila said to the bus driver as she jumped the last step off of the bus and ran toward her house.

"Wait up!" Leila's friend, Kait, yelled.

Leila sighed and slowed down.

"Want to do something fun?" Kait asked when she caught up.

"Sorry, can't," Leila answered, still on the move.

Kait continued as if she hadn't heard Leila. "I think I can make my brother play with us today. If not, I have an idea for a new way to spy on my sister. Or, hey, did I tell you about that video I saw of a five-pound gummy bear? Maybe we could . . ."

"I'm really sorry," Leila sped up again.

"Come on!" Kait struggled to keep up. "It can't be that important."

Oh, it was definitely that important. Leila had been counting down to this moment ever since math had ended at 10:30. That was five hours ago, and five hours is a really long time to count down to anything.

Her elderly neighbor Mrs. Crenshaw had promised to tell her about a super-old mystery and hidden treasure this afternoon. A hidden treasure! Just like the movies! Leila got butterflies in her tummy every time she thought about it.

"See you tomorrow!" Leila yelled over her shoulder as she ran up her driveway.

Inside the house, she hugged her mom, hugged her little dog, Nugget, and said the five magic words: "Wanna go for a walk?" Nugget leaped high enough to touch Leila's nose with his own. Leila smiled, clipped on the leash, and ran the whole way to Mrs. Crenshaw's house.

Mrs. Crenshaw had opened the door before Leila got to the porch. "Come in, Miss Detective! I've been waiting for you."

Nugget wagged his tail, hoping for a treat. Mrs. Crenshaw pulled a dog biscuit out of her pocket. "Yes, I've been waiting for you too," she said. Nugget wagged harder and stood on his back legs as Mrs. Crenshaw tossed him the treat. While Nugget ate his treat, Mrs. Crenshaw slipped on doggie slippers she'd bought him so he wouldn't mess up her floors.

Leila had sat at the kitchen table and opened her detective notebook to the unsolved case. "I'm ready!"

"I have cookies in the oven," Mrs. Crenshaw said. "Don't you want to wait until they're ready?"

"Nooo!" Leila pretended to melt in her seat. "You've got to tell me now!"

Mrs. Crenshaw laughed. "OK, OK, I suppose I owe you." She grabbed an old school yearbook from the counter and flipped through it until she landed on a black-and-white picture of a man with thick glasses, a thin mustache, and a gleam in his eye. "Do you know who this is?"

Leila shook her head.

"This is Mr. McGee. He was the first principal at Englewood Elementary School."

"That's where I go to school!" Leila exclaimed.

Mrs. Crenshaw smiled and nodded. "I went there too," she said. "Look." She flipped a few pages and pointed to a girl with tight curls and a smile that was almost too big for her face. "That little girl was never more excited for anything in her life than she was for June 4, 1947—the last day of third grade. That was the day of the treasure hunt."

Leila scooted forward in her chair. Finally, the good stuff.

Mrs. Crenshaw continued. "Mr. McGee was the best principal. There were more than four hundred kids in school, and Mr. McGee had nicknames for every single one of them. I was Nance, after Nancy Drew, because I was so good at solving mysteries.

"Mr. McGee loved mysteries, and he loved surprises. He loved them so much that a few weeks before my third-grade year ended, he announced that he'd have a special mystery for all the students to solve together on the last day of school. It would be a treasure hunt, and the student who found the treasure first got to keep it."

"What was the treasure?"

"Mr. McGee wouldn't tell anyone," Mrs. Crenshaw said. "It was probably just some little trinket, but people started saying that they'd heard Mr. McGee had buried a treasure chest under the playground,

or he'd inherited gold coins, or he secretly owned a toy store. One boy was even telling everybody that Principal McGee used to be a pirate."

Leila wrote "Pirate?" in her notes and looked back up.

Mrs. Crenshaw continued. "On the last day, everyone was buzzing. A lot of kids brought magnifying glasses or dressed up as Sherlock Holmes. The pirate boy wore an eye patch. We all gathered at the flagpole for our first clue. We waited and waited, but Principal McGee never showed up. One of the teachers finally got word that Principal McGee's wife was sick, and he had gone to the hospital with her in the middle of the night. The treasure hunt was canceled."

"But you were able to do it the next year, right?" Leila asked.

Mrs. Crenshaw shook her head. "Principal McGee moved across the country that summer so his wife could get better care. She eventually got better, but the McGees never returned."

Leila was starting to understand. "So the treasure stayed hidden."

"Everyone else forgot about it, but I couldn't," Mrs. Crenshaw said. "I looked all over the school for clues. I thought that if I could just find one, I'd be able to pick up the trail and solve the mystery. I stayed an hour after school for a month straight, searching classrooms, questioning teachers, and reading about famous treasure hunts. I even started digging in the corner of the playground before the janitor made me stop."

"But you never found it?"

"Nobody's found it."

"And you think I can find it? After all these years? With no clues or anything?!" This wasn't exactly the news Leila had been hoping for.

"I know it probably won't happen," Mrs. Crenshaw said. "The clues are almost definitely gone by now. I just remember how much fun I had treasure hunting, and I thought you'd enjoy it too. Mostly, I just wanted to give you a chance to look before it's gone for good."

Leila nodded. After all these years, Englewood Elementary was finally getting a new building. When Leila's bus passed the construction site for the new school every morning, she always strained to catch a glimpse of the progress on its gigantic playground. By June, the current school building would be nothing but a memory.

"OK," Leila sighed. "I'll take the case. It doesn't hurt to look, right?"

The mystery quickly sucked Leila in. Mrs. Crenshaw was right—treasure hunting was a lot of fun. Before Leila knew it, she was memorizing every half-clue and maybe-clue Mrs. Crenshaw had written down as a kid. She scoured every dusty corner and tall cabinet in the school for anything that looked old. She talked to Nugget so much about the case that even he seemed to tire of it.

After a few weeks of no clues, though, Leila's interest in the treasure started to fizzle. Sure, she wanted to find it, but she had to face the facts—the trail was gone.

Other cases started to crowd the treasure out of her mind. Every day, the new building was looking more like a school, and every day, Leila cared less that the old building and its treasure were going to be gone. After two months, Leila had all but forgotten the treasure hunt mystery.

That all changed the day she found clue number one.

CLUE NUMBER ONE

Leila wasn't even trying to find the hidden treasure the day she stumbled upon the first clue. She was working on a completely different mystery that morning—the Case of How to Stay Awake During the World's Most Boring History Lesson.

"And this is Millard Fillmore," Leila's teacher, Mrs. Pierce, said as she changed the picture on the screen. "He was the thirteenth president, and the first to have a stepmother."

Mrs. Pierce could make any lesson exciting—especially history—but even she was struggling with the "Presidents You've Never Heard Of" chapter. "And this is Grover Cleveland. He actually served two different terms in the White House. Can you imagine being president two different times?"

Yup. Leila could imagine it pretty easily. Her eyelids started drooping, so she concentrated on the picture of Grover Cleveland to stay awake. She stared at his bushy mustache and bowtie. She wondered what it would be like to have the name "Grover." Wait, was this the guy who discovered Cleveland? Her eyelids were getting heavy again.

Mrs. Pierce changed the picture again, and Leila gasped out loud.

"This is William Henry Harrison," Mrs. Pierce said. "He was president for the shortest amount of time—only thirty-one days."

Leila's hand shot up.

"Yes, Leila!" Mrs. Pierce said, beaming. She seemed happy that at least one person in the class was paying close enough attention to ask a question.

"Did William Henry Harrison have anything to do with our school?" Leila asked.

Mrs. Pierce looked confused. "Well, he died long before our school was built, and I don't think he ever visited our town. Why do you ask?"

"No reason!" Leila said, her face turning red. "Silly question!"

But it wasn't a silly question. Leila had seen the face somewhere before, and she was almost positive she'd seen it at the school. But where? It took her another two minutes to figure it out, and when she did, she gasped again. The girl in front of her turned around to give her an annoyed look. "Sorry," Leila mouthed.

With the building closing for good at the end of the school year, the principal had decided to dig up a bunch of old stuff from Englewood Elementary's history and display it in the hallways. Leila had spent hours studying the pictures and knickknacks because she knew they were probably her only chance of finding the clues that Principal McGee had hidden all those years ago.

One of the things she'd studied for a whole week was the staff picture collection. Every year, the school displayed a group picture of all the school's teachers in the hallway next to the office. Leila was never sure why the school did that—

maybe so students wouldn't forget what their teacher looked like?

This year, the school had lined an entire hallway with staff pictures going back to the 1940s. Leila spent the longest time staring at the 1947 picture to learn whatever she could about the year of the treasure hunt. Turns out, Principal McGee had hidden a very important clue in the picture.

The moment school let out, Leila ran for the picture. She had to see if she was right. When she got there, her breath caught. In the second row of the picture, among thirty serious teachers, someone had

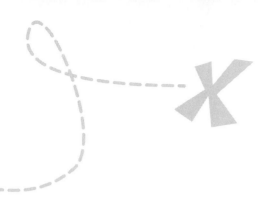

carefully pasted the face of a man who'd
died one hundred years before the picture
was even taken. It was President William
Henry Harrison.

HALL OF PRESIDENTS

When Kait sat next to Leila on the bus, she gave her friend a weird look.

"You OK?" Kait asked.

"Uh, yeah!" Leila said.

"Cuz you're doing that face that people make on *Scooby-Doo* when they've seen a ghost."

"Oh! Haha! Weird!" Leila wanted so much to tell someone about her discovery, but she knew that if she told Kait, the whole school would know in two seconds,

and she needed to keep this secret a little longer—at least until she could ask Mrs. Crenshaw about it.

Kait frowned at Leila like she didn't believe her, but she decided to drop it.

The two girls went their separate ways off the bus. Leila walked to her house like everything was normal, but as soon as she stepped inside, she started running.

Her mom tilted her head after Leila gave her the world's fastest hug. "What's got you so excited?" she asked.

"I just found a big clue," Leila said, fumbling with Nugget's leash. "A BIG clue! I've got to tell Mrs. Crenshaw."

Leila sprinted out the door, and Nugget matched her step for step. When she reached Mrs. Crenshaw's front door, she started knocking and knocking.

Mrs. Crenshaw came to the door, annoyed. "What?" she asked harshly before looking down to see Leila and Nugget.

"The first clue!" Leila gasped. "I found the first clue!"

Mrs. Crenshaw's face softened, and she opened the door. "The first clue to what, dear?"

"THE TREASURE!" Leila squealed, skipping into the house.

Mrs. Crenshaw's eyes got wide. Nugget ran into the house before Mrs. Crenshaw could put on his slippers and bounded around in glee—not that he knew what was going on, but everyone was so excited that he had to bound. After a full minute, both Leila and Nugget calmed down enough that Leila could finally tell Mrs. Crenshaw the whole story of her discovery. "Can you believe it?!" Leila asked when she'd finally finished.

Mrs. Crenshaw folded her arms across her chest. She looked like she wanted to believe it, but she wasn't convinced yet.

"Are you sure it was President Harrison?" Mrs. Crenshaw asked. "It's a blurry, old picture, and a lot of blurry, old pictures look the same."

"Very sure!" Leila exclaimed. "Surer than sure! If you look really close at the picture, you can see where Principal McGee cut around the president's head and glued it on there. But what could it mean?!"

"The Hall of Presidents," Mrs. Crenshaw said.

"What's that?"

"Principal McGee was very big on history, so he lined the whole east hallway of the school with pictures and facts about U.S. presidents—from Washington all the way to Truman. This must mean that the next clue is hidden behind Harrison's picture."

Leila's shoulders slumped. "But that picture isn't there anymore."

"Right."

"Oh."

"I'm sorry, honey. But that was an excellent job finding the first clue! In all these years, you're the only person who's ever noticed it."

Leila was too deep in thought to take the compliment. "But what if the clue's still there?"

Mrs. Crenshaw shook her head. "That picture of Harrison is long gone. Nobody's keeping a poster that old."

"But what if the clue wasn't on the poster? What if it was somewhere nearby?"

Mrs. Crenshaw shrugged. "Even so, it's not going to last all these years."

"This clue did!" Leila was warming up to this idea. "Do you remember where Harrison would have been in the hallway?"

"I could figure it out, but . . ."

"Please? Oh please, could you show me?!"

Even though Mrs. Crenshaw was shaking her head, a tiny sliver of a smile crept onto her face, giving her away.

Leila knew that Mrs. Crenshaw wanted to find this treasure just as much as she did. "Pleeeeease?"

Mrs. Crenshaw huffed. "My nephew's the school janitor. I suppose I could give him a call."

"Yay!" Leila danced around the room. "Nugget, we're going for a ride!" Nugget danced too.

Mrs. Crenshaw called her nephew, Leila called her mom, and five minutes later, they were ready to leave. Mrs. Crenshaw eyed Nugget as she unlocked her car. "He's not going to shed all over my seats, is he?"

"Oh no!" Leila exclaimed. "He's a cavapoo!"

"A what?" Mrs. Crenshaw asked with squinty eyes.

"Cavapoo! That means he's part poodle, so he doesn't shed!"

Nugget wagged his tail proudly.

Mrs. Crenshaw thought for another few seconds, then sighed. "I've never let a dog in my car before. He'd better watch himself."

"He will! I'll make sure of it." Leila scooped Nugget into her arms and sat on the spotless back seat of Mrs. Crenshaw's car.

Three minutes later, they arrived at the school. "OK, pooch, you watch yourself in here," Mrs. Crenshaw said.

"Oh no, we can't leave him in the car by himself," Leila responded.

"Why not?"

Nugget pressed his nose to the window, fogging it all up.

Mrs. Crenshaw rolled her eyes. "Fine, fine, fine. Tell him to stop snotting all over my windows." She opened the door to let Leila and Nugget out. "Keep him on a leash, and let me do the talking."

The janitor, Mr. Peterman, was taking down the flag for the day when Leila, Nugget, and Mrs. Crenshaw walked up. He looked down at Nugget. "Oh no, Aunt Margaret! You didn't tell me . . ."

"It'll be fine, Daniel," she said. "The dog's housetrained, and he's a something-poo that doesn't shed."

"Cavapoo," Leila added helpfully.

Mrs. Crenshaw didn't wait for permission from the stunned Mr. Peterman—she just took the key out of his hand and walked toward the school door.

Mr. Peterman ran in front of the door. "Aunt Margaret, I really can't let you go inside with the dog."

Mrs. Crenshaw turned toward her nephew with a stern stare. "Daniel, this is concerning a treasure inside the school. Now, if you . . ."

"A treasure?" Mr. Peterman's whole expression changed. "Oh! Um, OK. Just don't let anyone see you."

Mrs. Crenshaw nodded and unlocked the door. Once they were inside, Leila squealed. "I can't believe that worked!"

Mrs. Crenshaw allowed herself a small grin. "Daniel knows what's best for him." Then, she turned down a long hallway. "Harrison was the ninth president, so his picture would be nine doors down on the left."

Leila counted off the doors until they got to the music room. The three of them stared at a bulletin board decorated with smiling musical notes.

"This is it," Mrs. Crenshaw finally said.

"OK, so maybe the clue is underneath the decorations on the board," Leila suggested.

"It's not," Mrs. Crenshaw said. "This bulletin board wasn't even here when I was in school."

"So maybe it's on the wall behind the bulletin board!"

"For one thing, no. It's not. For another, I didn't bring my power tools to remove a bulletin board. Did you?"

Leila wasn't about to give up after coming all this way. "Well, maybe it's in the room behind the wall!"

Mrs. Crenshaw sighed. "We can check."

Leila, Nugget, and Mrs. Crenshaw spent the next half hour searching the music room. Nugget found lots of crumbs to gobble up, but that was about it.

Finally, Leila sighed. "I guess it's not in here," she said. "You were right, Mrs. Crenshaw. I just really wanted to find that clue."

"It's OK, dear," Mrs. Crenshaw said. "I did too."

They walked out to the hallway and stared at the bulletin board one last time. Nugget, who was still in crumb-finding mode, put his nose to the ground and started sniffing. He sniffed closer to the wall. Then, he suddenly started sniffing and pawing one of the bricks.

"Nugget!" Leila said. "Don't be bad! There's nothing . . ." She stopped in the middle of her sentence and got real close to the brick.

A thin line had been cut into the wall all the way around the brick. Leila tried pushing on the brick. Nothing happened. She pushed harder. Still nothing. Nugget stared at the brick with squinty eyes and a waggly tail. Leila sat on the ground, scooched Nugget out of the way, and kicked the brick as hard as she could.

CRACK!

It broke free, revealing a small hole in the wall. Inside the hole was a package.

THE OCEAN BLUE

Leila carefully pulled the package out of the wall and unwrapped it. Inside were a dozen ancient chocolate bars. Leila picked up one of the bars and turned it over in her hand. The wrapper read, "Bojo Bar! Fresh and Delicious!"

"A Bojo Bar!" Mrs. Crenshaw said. "I haven't seen one of those for fifty years!"

"What is it?"

"They were supposed to be the freshest chocolate bars because they used a red, see-through inside wrapper instead of the usual silver paper. I don't think the red wrapper did anything special to keep the chocolate fresh, but it made me believe Bojo Bars were the best, so they always seemed to taste a little better."

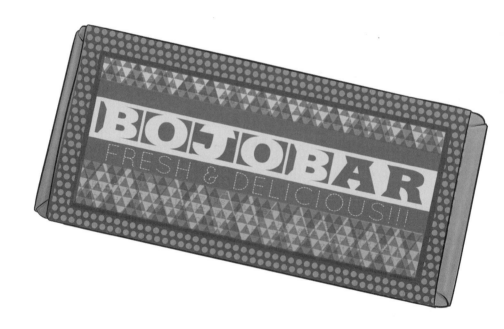

"I don't think it's fresh anymore," Leila said, noticing the expiration date was September 1949.

"Try opening it," Mrs. Crenshaw said. "Maybe there's a clue inside."

Leila made a face.

"Go ahead," Mrs. Crenshaw said. "It's just chocolate. It's not going to stink."

Leila held her nose just in case and carefully unpeeled the outside wrapper. Nothing but red plastic and an old candy bar inside.

"I don't get it," Leila said. "Does this mean . . ." Leila stopped in the middle of her sentence when she took a second glance at the outside wrapper. There was writing underneath. Leila's eyes got huge as she read the message.

Good job by you,
You've found clue number two!
Here's a treat
For you to eat
As you solve the mystery.

In 1492,
Columbus sailed the ocean BLUE.
But what would it mean
If the sea were GREEN?
Would it really change the things
you've READ?

Leila turned to Mrs. Crenshaw with the biggest grin on her face. "It's a clue! A real clue to a real treasure hunt! Eeee!"

Mrs. Crenshaw couldn't contain a little smile of her own. "Let's put the rest of these candy bars back into the wall and get out of here before my nephew calls animal control."

That night, Leila took twice as long as usual to finish her homework because her mind kept going back to the poem. On top of all her excitement about the clue, there was a little nervousness that she wouldn't figure it out in time. After all, there were only a few short months left in the school year.

The next day at school, Leila tried to concentrate. She really did. But no matter how hard she tried, she couldn't focus on the War of 1812 when all she wanted the teacher to talk about was Christopher Columbus. Things didn't get any better at lunch.

". . . afraid of the tree?"

Leila looked over. Kait was staring at her like she was expecting an answer to a question. "What did you say?" Leila asked.

Kait huffed. "Why was the cat afraid of the tree?" she repeated.

Leila gave her a weird look. "Why would you ask me that?"

"It's the riddle on my gummies!" Kait held up an empty wrapper. "I ask you my gummy riddle every day! What's wrong with you?"

"I'm sorry," Leila said. "I've just had a lot on my mind lately."

"It's like I'm talking to a zombie." Kait tapped Leila on the head. "You're not a zombie, are you?"

"Don't be a weirdo," Leila said. Zombie. Was that a clue? Zombies are green, right?

"You sure there's nothing you want to tell me, Ms. Zombie?" Kait asked.

"Uh, no." Leila felt bad about fibbing to her friend, but she'd just come up with an idea. She needed to visit the library.

Kait looked at her with squinty eyes for a second, then said, "Because of its bark."

"Huh?"

"That's the answer to the riddle. The cat was afraid of the tree because of its bark."

Leila still looked confused. "Oh."

Kait threw her head back and yelled her frustration to the ceiling. "Unnng!"

Leila looked at the clock and stood up. "Sorry, Kait. I've got to do something real quick."

"Probably eat some brains, right?!" Kait shouted after her. "Nice, juicy brains!"

Leila shook her head as she walked toward Ms. Jenkins, the lunch aide. She put on her best smile. "Excuse me, could I go to the library, please?"

"Sorry, not today," Ms. Jenkins said.

"Please? It's important."

Ms. Jenkins sighed and looked around the room until she spotted the janitor emptying trash. "Mr. Peterman! Can you take Miss Leila to the library real quick?"

Mr. Peterman was happy to take Leila. On the way, he asked, "Did you find that treasure yet?"

"No, but I'm getting close! Just need a few books about Christopher Columbus."

Once she got to the library, she was disappointed to find that there was only one book about Christopher Columbus, and it was a thin one for little kids. "I'm sorry," the librarian said. "Have you tried the internet?"

Leila sighed, nodded, and thanked the librarian. Mr. Peterman walked her to her next class in the music room. Leila's heart pounded faster as she neared the room. This would always be her own secret spot—the place where she . . .

Leila froze. The brick was gone, and the hiding spot was wide open. Leila bent down to look inside.

It was empty.

BOJO BARS

"Everything OK?" Mr. Peterman asked.

"What happened to that brick?!" Leila cried.

Mr. Peterman shook his head. "Was like that this morning. Probably some kids fooling around."

Leila started panicking. Who could have found the spot so fast? Had someone been watching her? Wait, was someone watching now?!

Amelia? Did Amelia just give her a weird look? Why was Chase digging in his book bag like that? What was he trying to hide? Leila spent the rest of the day trying to figure out who'd discovered her secret.

After school, Leila searched her house for listening devices. She didn't find any, of course, but she did throw away a spy decoder lens that had come free inside her cereal, which made her feel a little better. Then, she clipped a leash onto Nugget, and told her mom she was going to Mrs. Crenshaw's house.

Leila took twenty minutes to walk to Mrs. Crenshaw's house, zigging and zagging and spinning in circles the whole way. Nugget, of course, loved it.

When she was sure that nobody had followed her, Leila walked up the driveway to her friend Javy Martinez's house, then cut through his backyard into

Mrs. Crenshaw's yard. She snuck to her back door and knocked while looking over her shoulder.

Mrs. Crenshaw seemed surprised to see Leila at the wrong door. "What are you . . ." she started to ask before Leila ducked underneath her arm into the house. "What's going on?"

When Leila opened her mouth, a bunch of words spilled out in a jumble. "A spy! There's a spy following me, and I don't know where they're at, and I don't know if they put cameras in my house, or . . ." At that moment, Leila's eyes got even bigger, which seemed impossible because they were already really wide, ". . . or your house! We need to look for cameras right now! They could be listening to us!"

Mrs. Crenshaw snapped her fingers in Leila's face. "Hey! Hey! Stop talking nonsense. There are no cameras."

"But, but . . ." Leila was almost in tears by now. "But someone else found the second clue!"

"And?" Mrs. Crenshaw asked.

"And, well, isn't that bad?"

"No, it's not bad, and it certainly doesn't mean there's a spy," Mrs. Crenshaw said. "This isn't the movies. There aren't spies hiding cameras to win an elementary school scavenger hunt. As a detective, you've got to learn that the simplest answers are usually the right ones. Now, what's the simplest answer?"

"That someone hid a camera and . . ."

"Wrong," Mrs. Crenshaw interrupted. "The simplest answer is that my nephew saw you digging in the wall yesterday and took the weird bag of old candy bars to the office."

"Oh," Leila suddenly felt a little silly. "I guess that makes sense."

"And even if another student happened to find the clue, so what? This is a treasure hunt! Treasure hunts are supposed to have competition."

Leila sure didn't want any competition, but if Mrs. Crenshaw was right, then she was still the only one who'd seen the clue. She started to feel better.

That is, until lunch the next day.

"Oh brother," Kait said, shaking her head at her gummy wrapper. "This is a grandpa joke."

"A grandpa joke?" Leila asked, her mouth full of apple.

"Yeah, a joke my grandpa would tell me when I was little. It's that old. Don't they pay someone there to write jokes? That's the job I want when I get older."

"Well, what is it?" Leila asked.

"What's black and white and red all over?" Kait rolled her eyes. "So corny."

"Black and white and red?" Leila hadn't heard that one before. "Wait, don't tell me. I can figure it out."

"Sooo corny," Kait repeated.

"Is it like a zebra with . . ." Leila stopped in the middle of her answer because something across the cafeteria caught her attention. It was an older boy stuffing his face with a chocolate bar. Next to his hands, crumpled in a ball was the unmistakable, see-through red wrapper of a Bojo Bar.

Leila immediately stood up and started marching across the cafeteria. She'd found her spy, and she had a LOT of questions to ask him. The boy was much bigger than her, and she didn't know exactly what she'd say, but she wasn't about to let him get away with this. "Excuse me," she said when she arrived.

All eyes at the table turned to Leila. "Uh, can I help you?" the boy asked.

Leila held out her finger like a lawyer pointing at the bad guy in court. "Where did you get that?"

The boy looked confused. "This? Did she try to sell you one too?"

Now it was Leila's turn to be confused. "Did who try to sell me one?"

"It's actually pretty gross," the kid said. "She acted like it was some rare candy that was going to be the best thing I'd ever tasted, so I gave her two dollars for it. Two whole dollars for a single candy bar! What a rip-off. Don't let her trick you too."

"Let who trick me?" Leila asked. "Who sold that to you?"

The boy scanned the cafeteria, then finally found the candy dealer. "There!"

Leila spun around. He was pointing at Kait.

NEWSPAPER

When Leila made it back to the table, Kait was ready for her. "You figured it out, huh, detective?"

"Why would you spy on your best friend?" Leila asked.

"Why would you hide something from your best friend?" Kait shot back.

"I wasn't hiding it from you. I just wasn't telling you."

Kait blinked a few times. "That literally makes no sense."

Leila sighed. "How did you do it?"

Kait smiled a smug little smile. "You were clearly up to something the other day, so I got on my bike and followed you to that old lady's house."

"You know her name is Mrs. Crenshaw."

"Right, OK. So anyway, I waited outside for a few minutes, then just as I was about to give up and go back home, you guys got in the car. It looked like you were heading toward the school, so I biked there. When I finally got to the school, the janitor wouldn't let me in, but he told me that you went to the music room. The next day, I found the weird brick outside the music room, pulled it back, and ta-da!" Kait made a fancy motion with her hand and bowed.

"So you decided to sell the candy bars?"

"No," Kait said. "I decided to eat them. To get back at you. But they were gross, so then I decided to sell them."

"They were from 1947," Leila said.

Kait looked sick. "I did not know that."

"So you didn't care about the treasure?" Leila asked.

Kait looked at Leila out of the corner of her eye. "What treasure?"

"Do you have any of the candy bars with you now?" Leila asked.

Kait dug one out of her backpack. Leila peeled back the outside wrapper and showed her the riddle. Kait gasped. "What does that mean?!"

Leila looked around. "You can't tell anyone." Then, she told Kait everything about Principal McGee, the decades-old treasure, and the president in the picture.

By the time she finished, Kait was exploding with questions. "So there's a buried treasure right here in the school?!"

"Probably."

"And nobody knows what it is?!"

"Nope."

"So it could be gold or something?!"

Leila shrugged. "I mean, probably not."

"Yeah. It's a treasure. It's definitely gold. And you didn't tell me about this gold—why, again?"

Leila sighed. "Because you have a tough time keeping secrets, and I didn't want the whole school to know about it."

Kait gasped. "You wanted the treasure for yourself!"

"No!" Leila said. "I was going to tell you! I just didn't think you could . . ."

"I wouldn't have told anyone," Kait said. "You know why? Because you're my friend. And friends keep secrets for each other. But I guess that's not as important to you as some silly treasure." With that, Kait stomped away, leaving her lunch behind.

"Come on, Kait!" Leila shouted after her friend. She started picking up Kait's stuff to take back to her. Was Kait right? Should Leila have shared her secret earlier?

Leila was deep in thought when she picked up Kait's gummy wrapper and noticed the answer to the joke Kait had been trying to tell her earlier:

A newspaper.

A newspaper? Even though Leila had a thousand things on her mind, the answer made her stop. That didn't make sense. Newspapers are black and white, but they sure aren't red. Leila turned the wrapper over and read the joke for herself.

"'What's black and white and read all over?'"

Ohhh, now Leila understood. A newspaper is READ all over; it's not the color red. Funny. Well, not really funny, but funny in a grandpa-joke kind of way.

Leila crumpled the garbage and then cleaned up the rest of Kait's mess. But as she was putting the Bojo Bar back into Kait's backpack, the candy bar's see-through, red inside wrapper caught her eye. Leila held the Bojo Bar to her face.

"That's it!" she said to herself.

"Did you figure out the candy bar clue?" someone asked.

Leila's head shot up. Gwyneth Watson from Ms. Liggins's third-grade class was sitting at the next table, holding up her own Bojo Bar. "We've been trying to figure it out all lunch," Gwyneth said. "What do you think it means?"

Leila's heart started pounding. How many people were now looking for the treasure? She had to find Kait.

7

RUNNING SHOES

Leila ran into Kait pacing angrily in the hallway. "Kait!" She handed over the backpack. "How many of those candy bars did you sell? I think I figured it out, but we need to hurry because . . ."

Kait pretended that she didn't hear Leila and walked away in the middle of her sentence.

During science, Leila tried to get Kait's attention with Kait's favorite thing: a note. But when Kait opened the note and saw who it was from, she crumpled it up. On the bus, Leila tried to sit next to Kait, but Kait had already taken the seat next to Javy.

When Leila got home, she plopped on her bed and started talking to Nugget. "Errrg, this is so frustrating!"

Nugget put his head on her lap.

"I finally figured out the second clue, but I feel bad about going on until I make things right with Kait, you know?"

Nugget gave Leila's hand a little lick. He knew.

"I know I should have told her before; I just didn't want her to blab it to the whole school. But guess what? She somehow ended up blabbing anyways! Now, someone else might find the clue before I do! Should I just look for the clue now? Do you think Kait would understand?"

Nugget rolled over for a tummy rub. Leila started scratching. Nugget wiggled around until he found a cozy spot, then lay there with his eyes closed and tongue half hanging out of his mouth. Leila sighed. "Yeah, I know."

Leila got a few things together, walked to Kait's house and knocked on the door. Kait's mom answered. "Hi, Leila!" Then she looked down at Nugget, puzzled. "What's this?"

"Hi, Mrs. Korver. It's a message for Kait. Can I talk to her?"

"Kait!" Mrs. Korver yelled. "Nugget has a message for you!"

"Can't come to the door!" Kait yelled from upstairs. "I'm busy!"

Mrs. Korver shook her head. "Hold on," she muttered to Leila as she turned around. A minute later, she returned with Kait.

"What?!" Kait asked.

"Look." Her mom pointed.

Nugget was staring back at Kait with giant puppy eyes and a sign around his neck that said, "I'm sorry."

"So?" Kait asked.

"So you listen to her," Mrs. Korver said. "She's your friend, and she's trying to apologize."

Kait sighed, and her mom left.

"I'm sorry," Leila said.

"OK."

"No, I mean it. I had this secret, and I wanted it for myself. It felt special, ya know? But friends share stuff with each other, especially secrets. You're my best friend, Kait, and I should have shared this secret with you. I understand why you would feel hurt. Do you forgive me?"

Kait folded her arms across her chest. Nugget wagged his tail harder.

"Also," Leila added. "I think I figured out the riddle, and I was wondering if you'd help me look for the next clue."

Kait was trying to play it cool, but she couldn't stop her eyes from lighting up. "You figured it out?"

Leila nodded. "But you didn't answer my question. Do you forgive me?"

"Yeah, of course," Kait said. "You were probably right anyways. I mean, I do like to blab. Now tell me what the clue means!"

Leila smiled. "Well, first, we're going to have to go to Mrs. Crenshaw's house."

"Unnnng!" Kait made a face. Mrs. Crenshaw had yelled at Kait once a long time ago, and Kait had never forgotten it.

Ten minutes later, Leila, Kait, and Nugget were walking to Mrs. Crenshaw's house. They would have left earlier, but Kait had insisted on finding her fastest running shoes in case Mrs. Crenshaw tried throwing her in a pot of boiling

water and she needed to run away. When they reached the house, Mrs. Crenshaw opened the door and welcomed Kait by holding out her hand. "Hello there, I'm Mrs. Crenshaw."

Kait paused, then shook her hand. "Kait Korver," she said. "Uh, how do you do?" Leila knew that Kait wouldn't normally ask people how they do, but she probably felt like it was the right thing to say to someone Mrs. Crenshaw's age based on her experience with black-and-white movies.

"Korver, huh?" Mrs. Crenshaw said. "Interesting."

"Interesting?" Kait asked, alarmed. "Why is that . . ."

"I think I figured out the clue!" Leila blurted. She'd been keeping this inside for far too long, and she couldn't bear to hold it in any longer. She walked to the kitchen and took off her jacket. As she walked, she kept talking. "What's black and white and red all over?"

"A newspaper," Mrs. Crenshaw and Kait answered at the same time. "It's the oldest joke in the world," Kait added.

"Right," Leila said. "It's a good joke to tell someone else, because 'read' and 'red' are easy to confuse when you hear them."

"OK," Kait said. "So?"

"Remember the clue? 'Columbus sailed the ocean BLUE. What would it mean if the sea were GREEN.' The two colors were capitalized in the poem. Then I realized the third capitalized word might also be a color." She pulled the Bojo Bar out of her pocket and pointed to the inside wrapper.

"Ohhhh," Kait said. "It's red!"

"Would it change the things you've READ!" Leila said. "This red wrapper is the key to figuring out the next clue!"

"I don't get it," Kait said.

"The poem makes it sound like the red color would change things. That made me think of the spy lens codes they have on my cereal box. Do you know what I'm talking about?"

Kait shook her head.

"The back of the cereal box has a jumble of shapes and numbers that don't look like anything. But if you cover the picture with the spy lens you find inside the box, you can see through the mess, and a secret code appears. Well, the spy lens is just a colored piece of plastic like the Bojo Bar wrapper. So if this is a spy lens code, we need to put the red wrapper over a map of the ocean that Christopher Columbus crossed!"

Mrs. Crenshaw started clapping. "That's brilliant!" she said.

"But what map?" Kait asked. "Any map from back then has to be gone by now, right?"

"Gone from the school," Mrs. Crenshaw said. "But maybe not gone altogether." She disappeared into the living room.

"See?" Leila said. "She doesn't bite."

"No, she probably kidnaps," Kait muttered.

Mrs. Crenshaw returned a minute later. "Put your jackets back on, girls. We're going to find this map."

Kait's eyes got wide. Leila laughed. "Come on, Kait, it's OK." Kait shook her head and backed up, ready to use her running shoes. Leila looked back at Mrs. Crenshaw. "Maybe it would help if you told us where we're going."

Mrs. Crenshaw smiled at Kait. "I just called your mom. We're going to your grandmother's house."

THE ZOO

In the car, Mrs. Crenshaw explained why they were visiting Kait's grandma. "Kait, your grandmother and I have become quite close over the last few years because we both love books."

Kait made a face at Leila. Books were definitely *not* one of her interests.

"A few years ago, in one of our book clubs, I mentioned a book I'd remembered from my childhood—*Happy Birthday, Mr. Bunny*. It was the first pop-up book I'd ever seen, and I remember how magical it felt. I spent hours as a child opening and closing the pages to figure out all the folds that made the pop-up pictures work. Well, the next week in book club, your grandmother gave me that exact book! It was eighty years old, and some of the pictures had been ripped, but your grandma had taped everything back together, so it was almost as good as new. She said she'd found the book in her attic. Kait, did you know your grandma was the school librarian for forty years?"

"Mmhmm," Kait said. "It's all she ever wants to talk about."

"When the school got rid of old books, your grandma would get to take them home with her. She has quite a collection in the attic."

"Oh, I know," Kait said. "When I was little, my cousins and I would build huge forts up there with all the books until my grandma found out and made us stop."

"There's one book in particular that I asked her to look for. I hope she has it."

When they arrived, Kait's grandpa opened the door. "Pumpkin!" he said when he saw Kait.

"Poppy!" Kait gave him a hug. "Hey, Baxter!" she said when she noticed the old Scottish Terrier at her grandpa's feet.

The dog gave her a little tail wag, then his eyes got big when he saw Nugget bound toward the door. Nugget ran up to the elderly dog and jumped around him for a full minute while Baxter waited patiently.

Kait's grandma came down the stairs holding the biggest book Leila had ever seen. "Kaitie!" she said as she gave her granddaughter a hug. Then, she gave Mrs. Crenshaw an air kiss on both cheeks. "I found the atlas you wanted."

"That book is humongopotamus!" Leila exclaimed.

Mrs. Crenshaw nodded. "I think it was the biggest book at the school for a long time, right, Judy?"

"You're probably right," Mrs. Korver said. "I remember Principal McGee was so proud of it. It came from his personal collection."

Everyone gathered around the old book as Kait's grandma carefully opened it and started turning pages. Each page had a map of a country, complete with hand-drawn details and fancy lettering. Mrs. Crenshaw broke the silence. "I remember going to the library sometimes after school just to flip through this atlas and imagine traveling to the countries."

Kait made a face. "You read a book of maps?"

"Life was pretty exciting back then, huh?"

"There's something special about these kinds of books though," Mrs. Korver said. "It's too bad the school library can't buy them anymore. It just got too expensive, especially since students could find everything they needed online."

They kept turning pages until they got to a full spread of the Atlantic Ocean. Leila got a tingling in her tummy as she pulled out the candy bar wrapper. "Let's see what we've got!" Everyone huddled around while Leila carefully slid the wrapper over the page. Nothing popped out.

"Try it again," Mrs. Crenshaw whispered.

Leila did. Nothing. She sighed. "Maybe it's on a different . . ."

"THERE!" Kait squealed.

Leila looked down. "I don't see anything."

"That dragon thing! Go back to that dragon thing!" Kait was so excited that she was jumping up and down.

Leila slid the wrapper back down to the corner of the page. There it was! Hidden in the belly of a big, red sea monster was a small set of numbers and letters written in green—736.98. "Kait! You're a genius!"

Kait was grinning ear to ear. "A rich genius! We're getting $736.98!"

"That's not money, dear," Kait's grandma said. "It's a Dewey Decimal number."

Kait's grin turned into a frown. "Oh. Uh, what's that? Is it like money?"

Now it was Mrs. Korver's turn to frown. "The Dewey Decimal System? It's the number system used to organize books in the library."

Kait stared blankly at her grandma. "Oh."

Mrs. Korver groaned. "Where did I go wrong? In the Dewey Decimal System, the

700s are all books about art, and the 730s all have to do with sculpting. Now a book numbered 736.98 would be about . . ." Mrs. Korver looked at the ceiling for a moment. "Paper folding and origami."

Everyone stared at Mrs. Korver with their mouths hanging open. Even the dogs. "You just knew that?" Kait asked. "Off the top of your head?"

Mrs. Korver winked. "I was a librarian for a long time."

"So you think the next clue is in a book about origami?" Leila asked.

"There's only one way to find out!" Mrs. Korver said as she gleefully led everyone up to the attic. Once they'd all reached the top of the creaky stairs, Mrs. Korver clicked on a single light bulb. Leila gasped. It looked like every book that had ever been written was stuffed in the attic. Bookcases, shelves, bins, and boxes all overflowed with old books. "How will we ever find it?!" Leila asked.

"What kind of librarian would I be if I didn't sort this all by the Dewey Decimal System?" Mrs. Korver replied.

Two minutes later, they'd found the only origami book in the attic and started flipping through it. Kait used the Bojo Bar wrapper to look for another hidden clue. Leila searched for suspicious writing. Mrs. Korver inspected the checkout card. Nobody found anything until Mrs. Crenshaw made a suggestion.

"You don't think he used the bookmark secret, do you?"

Mrs. Korver's eyes lit up. "Kait, can you get a butter knife from the kitchen?"

"What's the bookmark secret?" Leila asked as Kait ran downstairs.

"When we were in school, the students had this little game where we would pass notes to each other by hiding bookmarks in the binding of big books. We all thought we'd kept it a secret from the adults, but Principal McGee was smart. He knew all of our tricks."

Kait returned with a butter knife, and Mrs. Korver carefully slid it down the spine of the book. "I think I hit something!" she said. Everyone leaned in as she pushed the knife farther and farther until a yellow piece of paper peeked out of the bottom.

"Eeeps!" Kait squeaked.

Mrs. Korver pulled the paper all the way out and held it up. It was a beautifully

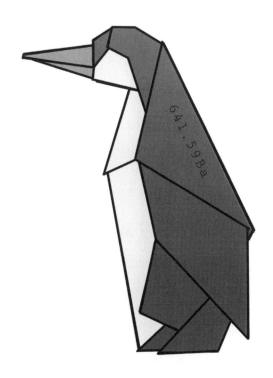

folded paper penguin with another Dewey Decimal number written on its wing. Kait squeaked again. "Where's this one?!" she asked.

"Should be a cookbook," Mrs. Korver replied.

Five minutes later, Mrs. Korver pulled a paper elephant from the spine of an old book called *The Handy Cookery.*

That elephant had another Dewey Decimal number on it that led them to a turtle in a history book, which led them to a snail in an astronomy book. Written on the snail was another poem. Mrs. Korver read it aloud for everyone.

You've completed your zoo,
On to the final clue!
If you're brave and strong,
You won't be wrong—
Just climb up, up, and away.

Mrs. Korver set the snail down and smiled. "Pack your gym shorts tomorrow, girls. I know where the final clue is."

THE FINAL CLUE

Leila and Kait were the first ones off the bus when it pulled up to school the next day. "Let's go, let's go, let's go!" Kait yelled as she ran inside.

Leila shushed her. "Right now, we're the only ones who know about this. We've got to keep quiet to make sure nobody gets to the treasure before us. Got it?"

Kait nodded, made a lip-zipping motion, and turned into the gymnasium. Leila followed her. Inside the gym, Leila pulled her dad's big binoculars out of her book bag and started scanning the rafters.

"See anything?" Kait asked.

Leila shook her head. "Your grandma said it was in the middle of . . ."

"Hey!" A voice interrupted them. "You girls need to get to class!"

Leila gulped. It was Mr. Glaser, the P.E. teacher. Mr. Glaser was the scariest teacher in school. He wasn't exactly mean, but he did kind of act like he was running an army boot camp most of the time. Plus, he used to be a football player, and even though that was a long time ago, he was still really big and muscle-y. Kait did the talking.

"Hi, Mr. Glaser," Kait said. "We're looking for the rope."

"The what?"

"The rope!" Kait repeated. "Ya know, the one that went all the way up to the ceiling."

Mrs. Korver had told the girls about a big rope that used to be in the gymnasium. Students would have to climb all the way to the top for P.E. class. Both her and Mrs. Crenshaw agreed that it was the worst thing they ever had to do in school.

"Strong and brave, climb up, up, and away . . ." The clue must have been talking about the rope.

Mr. Glaser looked confused. "The school cut that down twenty years ago."

"We know. We're just trying to figure out where it was tied. Do you remember?"

"I didn't work here back then."

"But you went to school here, right?" Kait asked. "Can you remember where it was when you were a kid?"

Mr. Glaser's patience was wearing thin. "Are you going to tell me what this is about?"

"A treasure," Kait said matter-of-factly.

"OK, you two need to get to class."

Kait crossed her arms. "And you need to return *The Secret of Wildcat Swamp*."

Mr. Glaser squinted at her.

"Thaaat's right," Kait said. "*The Secret of Wildcat Swamp*. Hardy Boys Book #31. You checked it out from the school library on November 3, 1984, and you haven't returned it yet. Even if we go by the 1984 fine rate of five cents per day, you owe $620.50. You've been running from the law for a long time, mister. My grandma is Mrs. Korver, the old librarian, and she sent me to collect. Of course, she's willing to forget about the fine if you help us find the clue."

Mr. Glaser rolled his eyes. "What is it?" he asked.

Leila explained the treasure hunt and the clue as fast as she could.

Mr. Glaser looked skeptical. "So you think there was some sort of clue at the top of the climbing rope?"

The girls nodded.

"I've got to tell you," Mr. Glaser said, "I climbed up there a bunch of times when I was a kid, and I never saw anything."

"Can you just look?" Leila pleaded. "It would make us really happy."

"And it would make you happy to not have to pay a $600 library fine. Mwahahaha!" Kait added.

"I'll look up there," Mr. Glaser said. "But only because your grandma was always nice to me." Mr. Glaser disappeared into the equipment room and reemerged a few seconds later pushing the Mover-Matic, an elevator platform he used to hang banners from the rafters and retrieve balls that had gotten stuck.

"See that hook thing up there?" he asked, pointing to the ceiling. "That's where the rope was." He locked the Mover-Matic into place and climbed onto the platform.

Kait's eyes got big. "Do you think . . ."

"Absolutely no kids allowed on the Mover-Matic!" Mr. Glaser said as he pressed a button and started rising into the air.

"Worth a try," Kait whispered to Leila.

Once Mr. Glaser made it up to the hook, he took a few seconds to look around. "No clue," he said. "I'm coming back!"

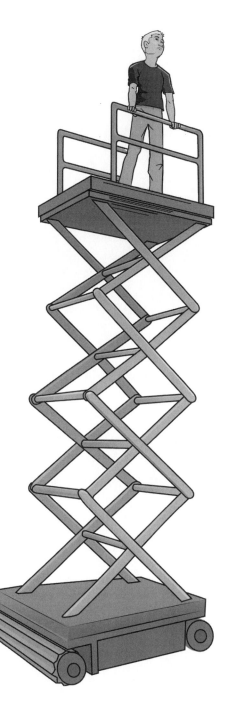

"Wait!" Leila yelled. "Keep looking! What else is around the hook?"

"Six tons of steel beams," he said. "I'm coming down." The platform started moving back down.

But Mr. Glaser did a funny thing after he pressed the down button. He quickly ran his hand over the steel beam. Even though he said he didn't believe in the treasure, even though he was giving up, even though he acted like Leila and Kait were silly for making him do this, there still must have been a tiny part of him that wanted to believe something was up there.

"Whoa," Mr. Glaser said after he felt the beam. He stopped the platform.

"What is it?!" Leila yelled.

Instead of answering, Mr. Glaser moved the platform back up to get a better look. He got real close, then peeled something off the top of the beam. "I don't believe it!" he said. "It looks like a note!"

The girls jumped up and down and met Mr. Glaser when the Mover-Matic finally reached the floor. "Thank you! Thank you so much!" Leila said.

Mr. Glaser shook his head. "I wouldn't have believed it if I hadn't seen it with

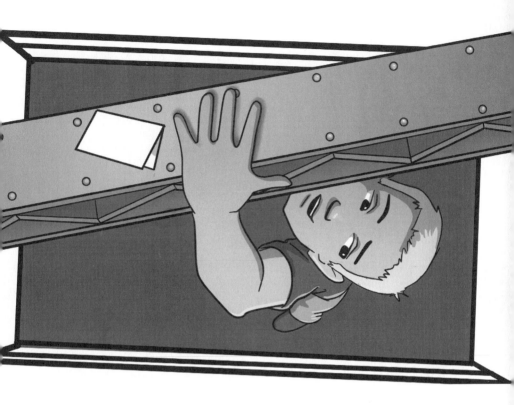

my own eyes," he said as he handed the
yellowed piece of paper over to Leila. Leila
carefully unfolded it and read it aloud.

Use your herd
To guess the magic word.
Then tell it to the man
Where it all began,
And the treasure will be yours!

The three of them were silent for a second. Finally, Kait asked, "What does it mean?"

"Yeah, what do you think it means?" a voice behind Kait repeated.

Oh no. Leila recognized the voice. It was Gwyneth Watson—the same girl who'd been trying to figure out the Bojo Bar clue the day before. She must have noticed Leila and Kait running off the bus and followed them to the gymnasium. With all the excitement of the final clue, Leila hadn't noticed her. Maybe she could convince Gwyneth to keep this little secret for just a bit longer. Leila started to turn. "Hi, Gwyn . . ."

She froze. Behind Gwyneth, waiting eagerly for her response, was half the school.

PINECONES

"What is that?!" someone asked from the crowd.

"A clue!" another voice answered. "A TREASURE CLUE!"

The crowd surged toward Leila to get a better look at the clue, which caused Mr. Glaser to snatch it out of her hand. "That's it!" he said. "Everyone get to class."

"But . . ." Leila started.

"Don't worry," Mr. Glaser said. "We'll put it up for everyone to see."

And just like that, Leila's small, secret treasure hunt had become the opposite of small and secret. By lunchtime, the whole school was searching for treasure—even some of the teachers! And if that weren't bad enough, Channel 5 News had gotten wind of the treasure, and they came to the school with cameras and everything. They interviewed Mr. Glaser, as if it was his idea to search the rafters.

Leila felt sick. She walked Nugget around the block three times after school that day, fuming the whole time. "It's not fair!" she said to Nugget.

He responded by sniffing a tree.

"After all that hard work, now someone else is going to find my treasure."

Nugget picked up a pinecone with his mouth, looked back at Leila, and tried to sprint ahead. He quickly dropped it, though, when he ran out of leash.

"Do you think there's still a chance?"

Nugget picked the pinecone back up and zigzagged for the next few minutes to keep Leila from stealing it. Leila barely noticed. She'd made up her mind.

"I'm going to find that treasure first because I'm going to work harder than everyone else."

And she did work harder than everyone else. Leila thought about the case every spare second of every day—even some non-spare seconds while she was supposed to be listening in class. Every day, she had a new clue to add to her notebook. Every afternoon, she had a new idea to share with Nugget on their walk. And every walk, Nugget had a new pinecone to steal.

Leila discovered that she had two big problems. One was that she had no idea what the "magic word" was. She figured it must have something to do with the origami animals because the clue mentioned "the herd." But no matter how long Leila spent staring at the animals or how many times she unfolded them, she couldn't figure out the magic word. Then, there was the bigger problem that "the man where it all began" had been gone for decades. Even if Leila did figure out the magic word, she couldn't tell it to Principal McGee. So what was the point?

The point was Leila had come this far, and she wasn't giving up now. So she kept looking and thinking and digging every day. Of course, she wasn't alone. The week following the discovery of the final clue was a full-blown treasure frenzy. Treasure clubs formed during lunch, hunting expeditions set out during recess, and teachers even canceled some of their classes so students could look for the treasure together. Although Leila was worried about all the new people looking for the treasure, she took comfort in knowing that none of them had the origami collection. She swore Kait to secrecy—neither of them could breathe a word about the animals to anyone. It was their only hope of figuring out the final clue first.

She didn't need to worry, though. Nobody even got close to finding the treasure. Soon, Leila was the only one looking again. The idea of a treasure right beneath your feet is fun, but actually searching the school and puzzling over clues for hours on end? No, thanks.

Even Kait, who'd been so excited to strike it rich in the early days, got bored. Every time Leila started discussing possible clues with her, Kait would try to turn the conversation back to what they'd do with all the money. She'd start talking about buying a five-pound gummy bear, then she'd wonder how much real-life CIA spy equipment costs, then she'd start rambling about her dream treehouse until Leila would finally give up on the conversation and go home.

Weeks and months went by. Now, every time Leila passed the new school building, she got sad instead of excited.

The beautiful windows in front and the giant playground in back were reminders that the clock was ticking on her treasure. The worst moment came during the last week of school. After turning in the final math test of the year, Leila plopped back in her seat, breathed a sigh of relief and looked out the window to daydream. That's when the sigh turned into a groan. Right next to Mrs. Pierce's third-grade classroom was parked a giant, yellow bulldozer.

That day after school, Leila hung her head during her whole walk with Nugget. "This is it," she said. "Summer vacation starts tomorrow, and then the treasure will be gone for good."

Leila sounded so sad that Nugget stopped sniffing long enough to come back and nuzzle her.

Leila smiled and bent over to pet him. "Thanks, little buddy."

Nugget let her scratch him for a few seconds before galloping off again.

"I thought for sure I'd find it," Leila continued. "Like, for sure, for sure. I never even cared if it was gold or money or anything. I just wanted to know what it was! That's the worst part. Now nobody will know what it is."

Just then, Nugget started sprinting. He'd found the pinecone tree. He grabbed the biggest one of the bunch, then ran ahead like normal. But this time, after just a few steps, he stopped. Instead of zigging and zagging and trying to keep the pinecone away from Leila, he turned around, walked back to her, and set the pinecone at her feet.

"Awww!" Leila put her hand over her mouth. "That's the sweetest thing ever, Nugget! That was so nice of you to share!"

Leila picked up the pinecone and stared at it for a minute. Then she glanced at Nugget again. He wagged his tail hard, as hard as he'd ever wagged it. Sharing that pinecone made him the happiest pup on the planet.

Leila bent down and gave her pooch a pat on the head. She knew what she needed to do now. She needed to be more like Nugget.

I PLEDGE ALLEGIANCE

"Attention!" Leila said when she stepped on the school bus the next day. "Attention, everyone!"

A few sleepy eyes looked her way.

"I want to invite everyone to help me search for the Englewood Elementary treasure today! We are stronger together than we are apart! Together, I believe . . ."

"Leila," Miss Carol said without turning around. "Can you please sit down so I can start driving?"

"Oh, uh, of course," Leila said.

As soon as she could, Leila got Kait and Gwyneth Watson to help her gather a group of kids together to share everything she knew about the treasure. She told them about President Harrison, the secret in the map—she even brought out the origami animals.

"Wait," Gwyneth said as she turned the paper turtle over in her hands. "You had these the whole time, and you didn't tell anyone?"

"I didn't either!" Kait said, proud of herself for not blabbing this big secret.

"I really wanted to be the one to find the treasure," Leila said. "But I realize now that I was just being silly. Every clue I found came because someone helped me. Mrs. Crenshaw, Kait, Mr. Glaser—even my dog!

So now I'm sharing this with all of you and asking for your help. Would you guys help me figure out the magic word?"

Everyone was on board. Mrs. Pierce's third-grade class was supposed to have an end-of-the-year party that day, but most of the juice and donuts went untouched because the entire class was working on the case. By ten o'clock, they'd organized into a code-cracking unit. Kait was at the front of the class with the pointer, tapping animal names on the board. "Penguin, Elephant, Turtle, Snail. What do those four animals have in common? They all have four legs, obviously, so . . ."

"Penguins and snails don't," someone interrupted.

"They all have four legs, EXCEPT FOR PENGUINS AND SNAILS, I was going to say," Kait said. "So that's suspicious. Also, all four animals have been to outer space, I think."

Students looked at each other, confused. "What if the paper animals come to life when you put them in a certain spot in the school?" one of the kids suggested.

"Have you tried cutting them?" someone else asked. "Maybe there'll be a clue if you cut them up and tape all the pieces back together."

People started shouting half-baked ideas over each other until the room was complete mayhem. Kait looked at Leila, threw up her hands, and walked to her seat. Leila shook her head. It was a good try.

Leila got up and walked toward the donut table. On her way, she passed

Benjamin Balmer, the quietest kid in class. Without a word, Ben walked to the front of the classroom, picked up a piece of chalk, and underlined the first letter of every animal—Penguin, Elephant, Turtle, Snail. Then he wrote the letters in order at the bottom of the chalkboard.

P-E-T-S.

The room went silent. Leila stared with her mouth open. That had to be it. After all those months, she couldn't believe she hadn't thought to do that. "Ben, I think you just figured out the magic word," Leila said.

The room burst into applause.

Ben was a hero for about five minutes until everyone realized that they didn't know what to do with the code word. With Principal McGee gone, what good did it do? The class tried chanting, "Pets! Pets! Pets!" a few times, until Mrs. Pierce made them stop.

After she'd quieted everyone down, Mrs. Pierce spoke to the class. "I'm proud of you all for working together to solve this mystery," she said. "Although it didn't lead to an actual treasure chest, you all discovered the treasure of teamwork today, and that's worth all the gold in the world. Why don't you give yourselves a hand?"

The class half-heartedly clapped. The treasure of teamwork? Yuck.

Mrs. Pierce smiled and continued. "It's almost noon, so let's clean up and head to the flagpole. Then it's off to summer vacation!"

Leila sighed as she threw away her trash and took her place in line. For her, the treasure hunt was always more about figuring out the mystery than finding a bunch of gold. And they'd solved the mystery, right? So why wasn't she more excited? Kait patted her on the back. "You did great."

When Mrs. Pierce's class walked outside and saw the scene at the flagpole, they all said, "Whoooaaa," at once. It looked like half the town was there. For as long as anyone could remember, it'd been Englewood Elementary's tradition for the students to gather on the last day of school for one final Pledge of Allegiance. With this being the last day for the old school, a bunch of extra people had joined the tradition this year. Parents, grandparents, and people who'd graduated decades earlier had all gathered to say goodbye to the old building. Mrs. Crenshaw was there, Kait's grandma was there, even the Channel 5 News crew had returned for the big occasion.

Principal Brown stepped in front of the crowd. "This is incredible," she said. "I know this school holds a special place in all of your hearts. As sad as we are to see it go, we are just as excited to make brand new memories in our new building this fall. Now, will you all join me as we salute the flag for one final Pledge of Allegiance."

Everyone put their hand over their heart and pledged as one.

"I pledge allegiance to the flag of the United States of America, and to the Republic, for which it stands . . ."

Leila looked around while she pledged. All the kids had giant grins on their faces as they tried to speed up the pledge so they could start summer break two seconds faster.

". . . One nation, under God . . ."

A lot of the adults looked sad. One or two even had watery eyes. Leila could tell the moment was bringing them back to their childhoods, when this simple tradition marked the beginning of a three-month adventure away from school.

". . . Indivisible . . ."

Wait a second. *Where it all began.* Leila's mind snapped back to the mystery, and her palms started sweating. She may have just figured out the whole thing.

". . . With liberty and justice for all."

All the students cheered.

"Thank you so much!" Principal Brown said over the commotion. "Have a safe summer!"

As the crowd dispersed, Mr. Peterman walked to the flagpole to take down the flag. Leila quickly followed after him. "Excuse me, Mr. Peterman?" she said.

He turned around. "Yes?"

Leila's heart was beating out of her chest. "Pets."

Mr. Peterman stared at her for a second, then a big smile spread across his face. He walked to the platform that Principal Brown had been speaking from and got everyone's attention. "Excuse me! Excuse me, everyone! I have one more announcement." He pulled Leila onto the platform with him and held up her arm. "This young lady just claimed the Englewood Elementary treasure!"

TREASURE WHEREVER YOU GO

One voice squealed above the noise of all
the confused people.

"AHHHHH!"

It was Kait.

"AHHHHHHHHHHHH!"

Kait pushed her way to the front of
the crowd to hug Leila. "ARE YOU RICH
NOW?! WHERE IS IT?! WHAT IS IT?!
WHAT HAPPENED?!"

Leila smiled. "Seeing everyone here for the Pledge of Allegiance today made me think of a line from the last clue. 'Tell it to the man where it all began.' Remember?"

"Of course," Kait said. By this time, Kait's grandma and Mrs. Crenshaw had also made their way to Leila.

"We always thought that part was talking about Principal McGee because he was the one who began the treasure hunt. But that's not what the poem says. It says, '*WHERE* it all began.' So it's talking about a place. And where was the treasure hunt supposed to have begun?"

"The flagpole!" Mrs. Crenshaw said.

"Exactly! So you're not supposed to tell the magic word to Principal McGee, you're supposed to tell it to a person who will be at the flagpole. And since it's the last day of school, that person is going to be the one in charge of taking down the flag after the Pledge."

Mr. Peterman wiggled his eyebrows. "Let me tell you all something that you're not going to believe," he said as he flipped through his keychain. "When you become the Englewood Elementary janitor, you get two things from the old janitor: a set of keys and instructions to unlock a cover at the bottom of the flagpole if—and only if—a student comes to you with the code word, 'Pets.' I always assumed that second part was a joke until that clue came out a few months ago."

"I can't believe you never told me!" Mrs. Crenshaw said.

"I'm sworn to secrecy, Aunt Margaret!" Mr. Peterman said. "It's the Janitor's Code!

Anyway, all that time went by with nobody claiming the treasure, so I just figured that it would be lost forever. Now, I can't wait to see what it is!"

Mr. Peterman finally found the right key, knelt at the flagpole, and wiped off some dirt to reveal a small lock. By this time, dozens of people had crowded around the scene, including one of the news cameras. "Do you want to do the honors?" Mr. Peterman asked Leila when he pushed the key into place.

Leila turned the key. She expected it to be hard to turn since the lock hadn't moved in decades, but it clicked right into place. Leila opened the cover, reached into the compartment, and pulled out a musty burlap sack.

"How much gold?!" Kait asked, trying to get a better view over Leila's shoulder.

"It's not that heavy," Leila said.

"Even better! Paper money!" Kait exclaimed.

Leila reached into the sack, and everyone leaned in closer. "It's . . . it's . . ." she grabbed a stack of something and pulled it out. "Baseball cards?"

"Baseball cards?" Kait exclaimed. "BASEBALL CARDS?!"

"I mean, they're pretty old baseball cards, so that's cool," Leila said as she pulled out more packs.

"That's not a treasure!" Kait said.

Leila reached back into the bag. "Wait, there's a box in here too!" Everyone leaned forward again as Leila pulled it out. "Oh, cool!" Leila said when she saw what it was. "It's an old doll!"

The Channel 5 cameraman sighed and lowered his camera. Real treasure would have been so great for TV ratings.

"Looks like there's a note taped to the back of the doll," Mrs. Crenshaw pointed out.

Leila opened it up. "It's one last note from Principal McGee!" she said.

The Channel 5 guy turned on his camera again.

Leila cleared her throat and read it aloud for the crowd.

Well done! You found the treasure.
You should feel pride beyond measure.
Now keep discovering! Continue learning!
Keep growing! Stay yearning!
And you'll surely find treasures
wherever you go.

"I don't get it," Kait said. "Does that mean there are like baseball cards and dolls all over the place?!"

Leila shrugged. "The best part of this treasure hunt wasn't the stuff at the end; it was all the clues hidden in plain sight. Maybe that's what Principal McGee was trying to say—if you keep your eyes open, you'll find awesome stuff all around you. What do you think, Mrs. Crenshaw?"

"I think you've figured it out again, detective."

Kait slumped her shoulders. "That's cool, I guess. I just think a mountain of money would have been cooler."

"Don't give up on that money mountain just yet," Mr. Peterman interrupted. He was holding the baseball cards. "These are 1947 Batter's Eye cards. They're rare, especially in perfect condition like this. This set has Ted Williams, Joe DiMaggio, Bob Feller—if you find a couple of the good

cards in these packs, you're looking at a
few thousand dollars easy!"

Kait gasped. "You are rich! I'm friends
with a rich lady! What are you going to do
with all the money?!"

Leila thought about it for a moment.
"Well, I don't really feel like it's my
money," she finally said. "It kind of seems
like it belongs to you and your grandma
and Mrs. Crenshaw and our whole class
for helping me with the clues. I wish
there was a way I could share it with
everyone."

"What about candy?!" Kait said. "You
could give candy to everyone! Or maybe
buy us all tablets or . . ."

"Books!" Leila interrupted.

"What?"

"Books! That's it! That's exactly the type of treasure Principal McGee was talking about!" Leila said. "Our school library isn't what it used to be, but we can fill it back up with all kinds of cool books for kids! What do you think about that, Mrs. Korver?"

Kait's grandma squeezed Leila. "I think that's wonderful, honey! Just wonderful!"

Kait looked up in the air. "Why do I have to be friends with such a nerd?!"

"Hey, I think we can keep a few dollars to buy something fun for us."

"Like what?"

Leila smiled and gave her own clue. "What's an animal that's chewy and gooey?"

"An animal that's chewy?" Kait gasped. "A gummy bear?!"

Leila started walking away.

Kait followed close behind. "A five-pound gummy bear?! Please tell me it's a five-pound gummy bear!"

Deserae and Dustin Brady are the parents of Leila Brady (a girl) and Nugget Brady (a dog). They live in Cleveland, Ohio. One time, Deserae found a huge spiral shell without any cracks on the beach, and that is the best treasure they've ever collected. If you live with a cute dog, Deserae and Dustin would love to see it! You can email your picture to dustin@dustinbradybooks.com.

April Brady grew up in Maine and has been bringing her imagination to life through pencil since she was a wee lass. Teaming up with her family to tell stories is her favorite thing to do. When she isn't drawing, she gets to have new adventures with her own little girls (the real Leila's cousins). If you like drawing your adventures or pets and family too, she'd be happy to see your art at aprilbradyart@yahoo.com.

Check out Leila and Nugget's
first mystery!

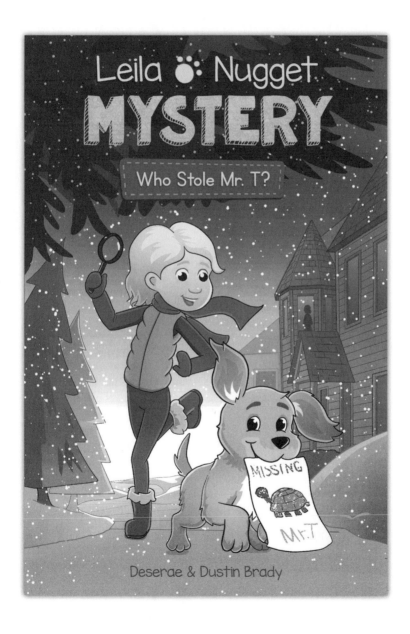

Andrews McMeel Publishing
a division of Andrews McMeel Universal
1130 Walnut Street, Kansas City, Missouri 64106

www.andrewsmcmeel.com

23 24 25 26 27 SDB 10 9 8 7 6 5 4 3 2 1

ISBN Paperback: 978-1-5248-7753-8
ISBN Hardback: 978-1-5248-7925-9

Library of Congress Control Number: 2022941123

Made by:
RR Donnelley (Guangdong) Printing Solutions Company Ltd
Address and location of manufacturer:
No. 2, Minzhu Road, Daning, Humen Town,
Dongguan City, Guangdong Province, China 523930
1st Printing—10/24/22

ATTENTION: SCHOOLS AND BUSINESSES
Andrews McMeel books are available at quantity discounts with
bulk purchase for educational, business, or sales promotional use.
For information, please e-mail the Andrews McMeel Publishing
Special Sales Department: sales@amuniversal.com.